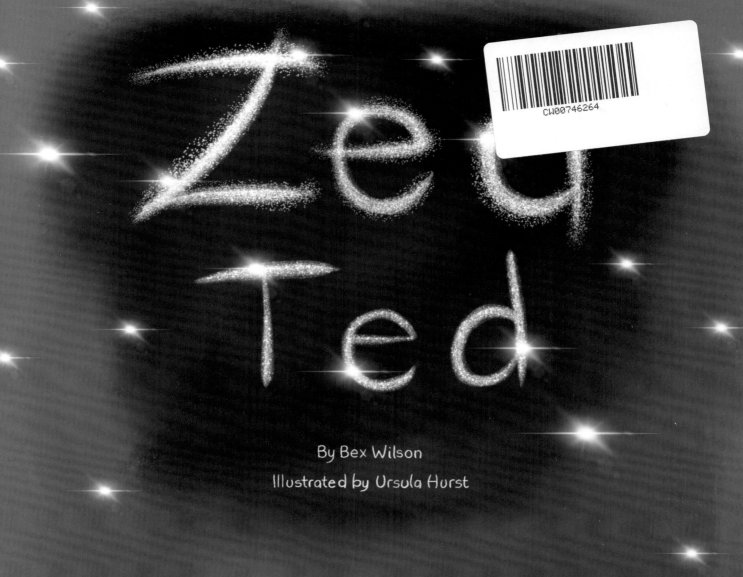

Zed Ted

By Bex Wilson

Illustrated by Ursula Hurst

All royalties go to…

Zarach
eat sleep learn

Delivering beds and basics to children in poverty

"Well, Zed Ted," announced Mama Bear, "today is your tenth birthday."
Zed Ted looked confused as he knew this and so did Mama. They had
already sung *Happy Birthday* and had his favourite breakfast of banana
pancakes!
Mama took a deep breath and continued, "So today, like all the Zed Teds
before you, your tenth birthday is the day when you must discover your Ted
superpower by going on a special journey."

The Ted family were a very famous family of Teddies that had ruled Roosevelt (the Land of the Teddies) for many happy years. Zed was the youngest member of the family and had heard *nothing* about Ted superpowers until now. He was bursting at the seams with questions.

What was a Ted superpower?
Who else had a Ted superpower?
How did he find out what his Ted superpower was?
What was a special journey?

All Mama Bear did in response to his questions was smile and say, "Only in the darkness can you see the stars."

And with that, she popped a red picnic backpack over his shoulders, ruffled his head, kissed his cheek, and sent him outside.

"Only in the darkness can you see the stars."
Zed Ted screwed up his face. This was not the birthday afternoon he had dreamed of. Where was he meant to go and what was he meant to do?

In the absence of a better idea, he set off to his favourite place, Roosevelt Hill Top Park. He decided that he would spend some time on the adventure playground, then head back home and ask Mama for another clue.

By the time he arrived at the park, he had eaten his sandwiches and was well into his packet of crisps. Sitting down on the swing, he tried to think. "Only in the darkness can you see the stars."

Zed must have said the words out loud, because, with a boing, a bouncy bear appeared and asked, "Are you on your special journey to find your superpower?"

Zed nodded eagerly, his eyes lighting up. This had to be a special visitor to help him with his impossible quest. The bear grinned.

"Nice to meet you, how do you do? Welcome to the Ted Power Supercrew. We may be small, but we aren't half mighty. Others feel good when they squeeze us tightly.

My name's Brownlee and I'm all about movement.

Get up and about and you'll see an improvement!

Stay still and lazy, and you'll struggle to smile.

I help people move for miles!"

Before Zed Ted could utter a word, Brownlee Ted, now with a curly spring on his t-shirt, had bounced off into the distance and Zed couldn't see him anymore!

Well, Zed was puzzled before, but now he was completely confused! He wandered over to the slide and began to climb the steps, repeating his one and only solid clue so far. "Only in the darkness can you see the stars."

Zed must have said the words out loud again, as with a fizz, a thoughtful looking bear appeared and asked, "Are you on your special journey to find your superpower?"
Zed nodded once again. This had to be another special visitor to help him with his impossible quest.

"Nice to meet you, how do you do? Welcome to the Ted Power Supercrew. We may be small, but we aren't half mighty. Others feel good when they squeeze us tightly.

My name's Malala and I'm all about learning.

Work hard at school, get your cogs turning!

Never absent, never late and your brain will soar,

Create, discover, investigate and explore."

Zed didn't even try to ask questions, as he knew Malala Ted would be gone before he could get his words out.

She was, but not before he saw a book appear on her t-shirt.

He screwed his face up tight again, trying to muster up his best thinking. After all, wouldn't it be wonderful to have a superpower just like the rest of the crew. If only he knew what his was. Focussing hard, he tried to remember who he had met so far: Brownlee, whose superpower was helping others to move more, and Malala, whose superpower was all about learning at school and trying hard.

What could his own Ted superpower be?

"Only in the darkness can you see the stars." Zed said the words out loud on purpose this time, hoping for another special visitor.

As soon as the final word was spoken, with a hoot, a very strong and healthy-looking bear appeared and asked, "Are you on your special journey to find your superpower?"
Zed gave the new bear a thumbs-up.

Roosevelt Hill Top Park had never been so busy!

"Nice to meet you, how do you do? Welcome to the Ted Power Supercrew. We may be small, but we aren't half mighty. Others feel good when they squeeze us tightly.

My name's Marcus and I'm all about food,

Without it we get poorly, moody and rude.

Everyone has the right to a healthy diet.

I help people speak out, not stay quiet."

Marcus touched his chest and stood proudly, as a picture of a rainbow made up of all kinds of fruit and vegetables lit up on his Ted t-shirt.

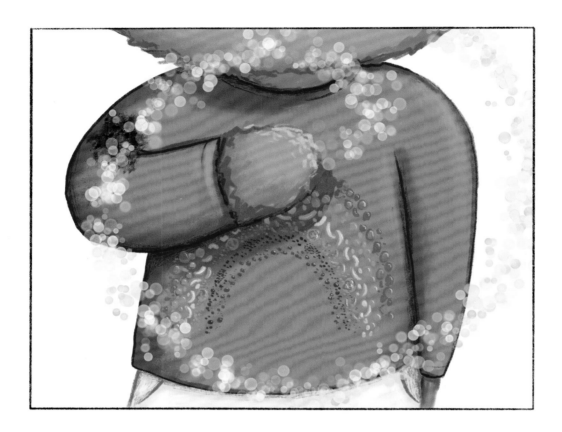

As Zed looked out to the horizon from the top of the slide, where he still sat, Marcus Ted disappeared into the distance at a sprint.

It was beginning to get dark now. Zed Ted had eaten all his food and been on all his favourite park equipment… twice! He couldn't possibly go home without an answer.

Deciding that there was nothing better to do, he attempted to summon a final visitor. "Only in the darkness can you see the stars."

Suddenly, with a bubbly whoosh, a smiley-looking bear appeared and asked,
"Are you on your special journey to find your superpower?"
Zed gave a friendly wave, "Yes, sireee," and awaited the happy bear's rap.

"Nice to meet you, how do you do? Welcome to the Ted Power Supercrew. We may be small, but we aren't half mighty. Others feel good when they squeeze us tightly.

My name's Meghan and I'm all about being kind.

We must think hard before we speak our mind.
Is it helpful? Is it hurtful? We must think and decide.

Give out kindness in buckets, create smiles with pride."

With a final flash of her beautiful smile, three love hearts appeared on Meghan Ted's t-shirt, one red, one blue and one yellow.

Then she was gone and Zed Ted was alone once more.

The sun began to fade on Zed's birthday. Silently, he sat pondering the events of the day and sighed, feeling sad that he was no closer to discovering his Ted superpower. This had been his worst birthday ever. He let out a long yawn and stretched his arms above his head, wishing he was at home in his lovely, warm bed. Glancing up, he could now see the stars, as it was dark.

All of a sudden, his tummy began to feel warm and, when he looked down, a huge colourful 'Z' had appeared on his t-shirt. What could this mean, he wondered.

And with a boing, fizz, hoot and a bubbly whoosh, Zed Ted had finally completed his impossible mission and had the answer to his special journey.

All the rest of the Supercrew and Mama Bear appeared at the park. They were cheering, whooping, clapping, and banging on pots and pans. Zed Ted took a deep breath and performed his very own rap for the first time.

"Nice to meet you, how do you do? Welcome to the Ted Power Supercrew. We may be small, but we aren't half mighty. Others feel good when they squeeze us tightly.

My name's Zed and I'm all about dreaming.

Bedtime rules 'cos sleep keeps you beaming.

Everyone can dream big if they have a good rest.

Getting lots of shut-eye keeps us at our best."

Eventually, after lots of celebrating and several rap-offs with his new crew, Zed Ted went to bed, on time, and his mum tucked him in.

"Mama, can I ask you something?" said Zed, as his eyelids began to feel heavy. "I'm still not sure what the clue you gave me meant."
Mama Bear smiled and started to explain, just as her mum had explained to her 25 years earlier, and just as Zed would explain to his children in years to come.

"A very wise man once pointed out that it's only when things seem at their worst, that you can find the beacons of light in your world, which can help steer you back on course. So, when things seem really tough in life, always know that all is not lost."

And with that, Zed drifted off to sleep thinking about how he could help other Teds understand the importance of quality sleep and dreaming big.
And he did just that.